A Gift from the Endowment for

Katherine Eldridge Muller

To Patricia Cummings

Simon & Schuster Books for Young Readers

An imprint of Simon & Schuster Children's Publishing Division

1230 Avenue of the Americas, New York, New York 10020

Copyright © 1956 by Oxford University Press

Copyright © renewed 1984 by Corgi Cottage Industries, L.L.C.

First Simon & Schuster Books for Young Readers edition, 2000

Printed in Hong Kong

1   3   5   7   9   10   8   6   4   2

Library of Congress Cataloging-in-Publication Data

Tudor, Tasha.

1 is one / by Tasha Tudor.

p.   cm.

Summary : Rhyming verse and pictures introduce the numbers from one to twenty.

ISBN 0-689-82843-8

[1. Counting. 2. Stories in rhyme.] I. Title. II. Title: One is one.

PZ8.3.TiAad 2000   [E]–dc21   99-31290   CIP

1 is One

By
TASHA TUDOR

Simon & Schuster Books for Young Readers

1 is one duckling

swimming in a dish

2 is two sisters

making a wish

3 is three swallows

up in the sky

4 is four sheep

nibbling rye

5 is five eggs

in a pretty round nest

6 is six children

all dressed in their best

7 is seven apples

on a little apple tree

8 is eight daffodils

you are picking for me

9 is nine red cherries

on a white china plate

10 is ten numbers

Tom has written on his slate

11 is eleven girls

dancing in a ring

12 is twelve baby birds

learning how to sing

13 is thirteen candles

upon a birthday cake

14 is fourteen mallard ducks

swimming on a lake

15 is fifteen roses

being made into a wreath

16 is sixteen rabbits

playing on a heath

17 is seventeen gourds

hanging up to dry

18 is eighteen stars

twinkling in the sky

19 is nineteen flowers

that little Jane has drawn

20 is twenty geese

flying toward the dawn